In the Middle of Fall

BY Kevin Henkes

ILLUSTRATED BY Laura Dronzek

GREENWILLOW BOOKS
An Imprint of HarperCollinsPublishers

Acrylic paints were used to prepare the full-color art.
The text type is 32-point Bernhard Gothic SG Medium.

Library of Congress Cataloging-in-Publication Data

Henkes, Kevin, author. | Dronzek, Laura, illustrator.
In the middle of fall / by Kevin Henkes ; illustrated by Laura Dronzek.
First edition. | New York, NY : Greenwillow Books, an imprint of
HarperCollinsPublishers, [2017] | Summary: "Introduces concepts and vocabulary of
fall—autumn colors, changes in plants and animals . . . and wind, which soon leads to the
next season"—Provided by publisher.
LCCN 2016023553 | ISBN 9780062573117
(trade ed.) | ISBN 9780062573124 (lib. bdg.)
Subjects: | CYAC: Autumn—Fiction. | Seasons—Fiction.
LCC PZ7.H389 In 2017 | DDC [E]—dc23
LC record available at https://lccn.loc.gov/2016023553

17 18 19 20 21 SCP 10 9 8 7 6 5 4 3 2 1
First Edition

Greenwillow Books

For Will and Clara

In the middle of Fall,
when the leaves
have already turned

and the sky is mostly gray
and the air is chilly

and the squirrels are frisky

and the gardens are brown

and the pumpkins are ready

and the apples are like ornaments,

it takes just one big gust of wind

and all at once—

everything
is yellow
and red
and orange

all over
all around

right in the middle of Fall.

But remember it

because soon . . .

the yellow
and red
and orange
will be gone

and the sky will change again

and then soon

very soon

the sky will be white and empty—

ready to fill up with snow.